June the Tiger

June the Tiger

by
John Fort

Illustrated by
Bernice Loewenstein

Little, Brown and Company
BOSTON   TORONTO

FIRST EDITION

т 11/75

Library of Congress Cataloging in Publication Data

Fort, John.
  June the Tiger.

  SUMMARY: When old Mrs. Pinckney's house is attacked by a marauding bear, her mangy dog, June the
Tiger, goes off with the local hero, Billy the Bull,
to take revenge on the culprit.
  [1. Dogs—Fiction. 2. Bears—Fiction] I. Loewenstein, Bernice. II. Title.
PZ7.F78Ju   [Fic]   75-12603
ISBN 0-316-28925-6

Published simultaneously in Canada
by Little, Brown & Company (Canada) Limited

PRINTED IN THE UNITED STATES OF AMERICA

To my father, Tomlinson Fort

Chapter One

Once upon a time in the early days of our Republic, there was, on the edge of a great swamp, a little cottage surrounded by a white picket fence. Until noon the fence appeared to be made more of morning glories than of wood and whitewash, and the cottage, though in need of a fresh coat of paint and with a shutter or two out of place, bore the burden of its years with a comfortable grace. The yard looked rather better grown than mown. Clumps of Queen Anne's lace and daffodils grew undisturbed. In the summer scuppernongs hung on an arbor and an old persimmon tree which stood in the back was a favorite spot for possums in the fall.

The swamp was known as Coolewahee. Once, Indians had paddled silently through the still, black waters to see the snowy egret. But now the vast forest of cypress and tupelo had few intruders. Some feared the swamp, others simply feared the unknown. There were a few, however, who understood the majestic beauty of the cloistered passageways, the fields of wild iris, the unhewn timber, and above all the wild creatures who dwelt there. To these few, the swamp was a friend.

In the little cottage there lived an old lady. Her name

was Mrs. Pinckney and her gentle manner and quiet
dignity presented a delightful contrast to the wildness of
the swamp. She had a kind face and her long white hair
was kept in place atop her head by a beautiful tortoiseshell
comb. Her dresses were long and of a style that was a
little out of fashion, but she wore them with a flourish
and in spite of their mended appearance, Mrs. Pinckney
could look quite grand. She had lived beside the swamp
for a long time, and in spite of some hardship, her ready
wit and enthusiasm for life had increased with the years.

4

Mrs. Pinckney loved the swamp and the cottage, and she had the devoted respect of all who knew her.

Mrs. Pinckney owned a cow, lots of chickens, a sow with pigs, and had her own garden, which she had planted all by herself. In her gardening getup, which included an old sunbonnet and a baggy pair of men's trousers, she could have frightened a scarecrow, but she was a regular demon with a hoe. She would laughingly compare herself with John the Baptist. "I'm just preparing the way," she would say. Tomatoes all summer and greens in the winter: there was plenty for all, including the deer and rabbits, who usually helped themselves.

Mrs. Pinckney was a wonderful cook. "I wonder who may stop by?" she would say, and soon the kitchen would be full of glazed ham and sweet potato pie, chicken pilau, muscadine jelly, and perhaps a white rose cake for dessert. Divinity candy was her specialty and at Christmastime she would make a box for every child she knew.

At times the cottage looked like an animal hospital. Mrs. Pinckney loved every wild creature, and there was always an injured bird being nursed to recovery in the kitchen or some poor baby that had lost its mother huddled in the parlor. She raised a fawn once and called it Billy and a certain coon still came scratching at the door looking for a handout or a warm snooze by the fire. During the day Mrs. Pinckney would chatter with the birds as if they were sharing the choicest gossip, and at teatime a titmouse always came for crumbs.

Mrs. Pinckney slept in an upstairs bedroom and it was here that she kept her most prized possession. Not that she spent an excess of time in it, but she was truly fond of her feather bed. It was a large four-poster, of a Spanish design, and long cherished by the Pinckney family. As evening drew on, Mrs. Pinckney would snuggle deep into the soft feathers and often a great owl who lived nearby would ask

Whoo, Whoo
I cooks for my folks,
Who cooks for you?

Life was very peaceful for Mrs. Pinckney and I

daresay it would have remained that way, if it had not been for June the Tiger.

Chapter Two

June the Tiger was a dog. Not an ordinary dog, to be sure, but all the same, a dog. As best could be remembered, he just showed up at Mrs. Pinckney's cottage one day about as unannounced as the preacher. Where he'd come from, no one knew. A long way off no doubt because he was footsore and tired. It was raining, and he scratched at the door, demanded to be let in, and headed straight for the kitchen, where Mrs. Pinckney laid out a plate of ham scraps and buttermilk that were left over from breakfast. "He'd been wandering like Moses, looking for the Promised Land," Mrs. Pinckney would say later. It didn't take Tiger half a minute to see that this was the spot for him. His traveling days were over at last. Mrs. Pinckney didn't have to pick him — he picked her.

"What a mug," Mrs. Pinckney would say affectionately. To everyone else he was as ugly as an old turkey neck, but to her, well, she thought he looked just fine. His hair was a mass of cowlicks, each looking as if it had been slept on the wrong way, and his color varied daily depending largely on the particular puddle he'd been in most recently. He wasn't big — about as big as a big coon, I guess, but lord, goodness he was tough. He wasn't easy to catch either, and if ever you got your hands on him, it was like grabbing a roll of barbed wire.

The way that dog loved Mrs. Pinckney soon became a legend. He kept as close to her as possible, and would follow her about the yard while she was at her gardening, never letting her out of his sight. Strangers weren't allowed within a mile of the house, and I daresay June the Tiger would have eaten alive anyone trying to harm Mrs. Pinckney. He had watched her cook so many times that he knew each recipe by heart, and from his favorite spot by the kitchen stove he could see every sausage hit the pan.

If June the Tiger could only have behaved himself, people probably would have gotten used to the way he looked, but that was not his way. Smart! "Why dadburn his hide," Sammy Bailey would say, "both my brothers-in-law put together aren't half as smart as that dog." In one trip to Perry's store he could start a dozen dogfights, and not be involved in any one of them, steal the day's supply of sliced bacon, cause at least two mules to kick loose from their traces, and much to the delight of the boys, attack Lizzie Belle Parsons' dress with sufficient vigor to expose her red pantaloons.

Mrs. Pinckney had at first called the dog June, but

the name didn't suit him at all, and after a couple of trips to the store he was not only the talk of the county, but quickly dubbed "the Tiger," or "June the Tiger." The name stuck, and as such was he known ever after.

The Tiger possessed a singular lack of respect for many of the traditional institutions of society. He amazed the world with his own particular combination of bravery and foolishness. Once, when the bishop was in church for one of those special services that bishops always come to, June the Tiger slipped into the balcony, waited until the invocation, then set up a howl that sounded like a chorus of spirits. One fat lady, Mrs. Thelma Whaley, I believe, leaped from the balcony. She was unhurt, thank

goodness, but her howls of indignation were not to be denied, and she quickly had half the congregation ministering to her imaginary wounds. A deacon broke his toe trying to catch June the Tiger, and a fight quickly broke out between the boys from Coolewahee Swamp and the Adams Run crowd. Mrs. Pinckney was secretly a little put out that everyone would carry on so over a little dog, but she acted distressed enough, and divided her time equally between Mrs. Whaley and the deacon with the broken toe. The bishop was finally able to bring the church to order; which he did by pronouncing a sentence of doom on June the Tiger, and canceling the service until the following Sunday.

They never did catch June the Tiger for this or any other of his mischievous acts. He'd always escape somehow and head straight for Mrs. Pinckney's, where he knew he was safe. And for all the trouble he caused, June the Tiger never did a really mean thing; in fact, his pranks provided some welcome excitement in a quiet country community.

It's true enough that there was a lot of tomfoolery connected with June the Tiger, but upon one subject he was all business. So much so, in fact, that it came close to being the ruin of him. For in those days black bears were still to be found in southern swamps, and if ever a dog hated bears, it was June the Tiger.

Chapter Three

Bears! That's right. And one bear in particular. He was known as Old Scratch and never had the Coolewahee district known such a dangerous and destructive beast. There were few of the nearby country folk who had not suffered from his onslaughts. Some had lost cattle and hogs, while others had had whole corn crops trampled just for the sake of meanness. All attempts to track him down had been unsuccessful. It was widely held that Scratch was a kind of monster that could not be killed, and that his evil temper was the result of witch's brew. These were only tales, of course, and not a bit of truth to them, but they greatly increased the fear in which the bear was held, and soon his reputation had spread throughout the county.

June the Tiger had been living with Mrs. Pinckney only a short time when first he ran into Old Scratch, and as it turned out, each grew to hate the other. Tiger, when not up to one of his many mischiefs, would think of little but the bear. All he wanted was one chance to knock the gizzard, chops, and daylights right out of him and he was sure that the next time he got hold of Scratch, all he would need for bear stew was a few potatoes. Down in the swamp Old Scratch was as mean as a skinny snake and as he rambled about he would uproot huge trees in a frightening display of temper over that rascally dog.

Their actual encounters were few, and as it happens, occurred only under the most unusual circumstances. Old Scratch was infected with a rheumatism that bothered him only on the very wettest and stormiest nights. On these nights the pain of the rheumatism would stir up his naturally melancholy disposition to a point beyond which he lost his fear of man. Then, with the wild night swirling about him, the huge black bear would make his

way out of the swamp and up the road that led to Mrs.
Pinckney's house.

On nights like these, if June the Tiger slept at all, it
was with one eye open and an ear cocked. As soon as the

bear reached the edge of the swamp he would stop and give a holler to let June the Tiger know he was coming. It was a kind of low singsong chant which, when caught by the wind, sounded like a great mournful sigh:

June, June the Tiger
June, June be wary . . .

The sound would increase in both pitch and volume with each repetition, and as the bear lumbered up out of the swamp he would stop every so often, listen, and repeat his eerie song:

June, June the Tiger
June, June be wary . . .

A dog's hearing is extremely keen, so that Scratch would no sooner let out his first good holler than June the Tiger would be out of the house and down the road to meet him. The ensuing fight, although always having the same outcome, was certainly a sight to see. The old bear would rear up on his hind legs and let out a roar that would stop most dogs dead in their tracks. But June the Tiger, sounding all the while like a whole kennel full of fice dogs, would run in and nip him a dozen times before the bear knew what hit him. In spite of his strength and

17

size, Old Scratch was no match for June the Tiger. That mutt could fight like a sack full of wildcats and was faster than a striped lizard crossing a dusty road. When the bear would turn one way, June the Tiger would be at him from the other side. Tiger did get hit by one of those monstrous paws once, and he took off like he'd been fired out of a homemade cannon. He sailed through the air and landed plumb near halfway to town. He'd never have found the fight again if Old Scratch hadn't been making such a fuss, and as it was, it was a good five-minute run back.

The fights never lasted long. The bear would soon realize he'd had more than enough of June the Tiger, and turn and head for the swamp. It wasn't an easy trip though, for June the Tiger would be right at his heels the whole way, and it would be a sore and angry bear who finally reached the safety of the swamp.

June the Tiger was always too smart to let Scratch lead him into the swamp, so, dripping wet and still fairly alive with excitement, he would trot back home to a warm spot by the fire and a good scolding from Mrs. Pinckney, who, not being the sort of person to think much about bears, had no idea what he had been up to.

Chapter Four

Twice a year Mrs. Pinckney went to visit her sister who lived in town. Mrs. Pinckney seldom left her little cottage, and on those rare occasions when she did, it was usually to call on friends nearby, but to visit her sister required a day's buggyride and she would be forced to spend the night away from home.

The prospect of such a trip always excited Mrs. Pinckney, and there was much stirring about in preparation.

Anyone who didn't know her would have thought she was catering to a grand party, for the buggy was overflowing with all the food she was bringing to her city friends. There were great boxes of fresh squash and okra, a whole side of smoked bacon, a basket of guinea eggs, jars of artichoke relish, and toasted pecans tucked everywhere.

Mrs. Pinckney had a fine team of horses. They were a handsome pair of grays named Daisy and Darling, who had been given a lot more sugar and a lot less of the whip than was probably good for them, but with Mrs. Pinckney at the reins they seemed to move along somehow. All the packing was finished and Mrs. Pinckney was struggling to hitch up the team when who should come riding up but Billy the Bull.

Did I say Billy the Bull? Why, bless me. I think I did — and you not knowing Billy the Bull from a bunch of collards. I can tell you that in those days folks knew Billy well, and many a man stepped lightly when he was around.

Not to say that Billy was a roughneck or a bully. Not a bit of it — a gentleman born he was, and smart as a new dollar, too. But Billy could not stand cussedness or ill-natured behavior, especially in the presence of ladies; and when such did occur — well, look out! I once saw a rowdy who had been rude to a lady get shook so hard that both his teeth and his pants fell off at the same time.

Need I say that Billy was quite a favorite? There wasn't a gal in petticoats who didn't have her eye out for him. The young ones loved him and the old ones thought him a saint. Yes, he was the pride of the county, and there was talk about him being governor someday.

But Billy had little mind for courtin' and less for politics. He spent most of his time roaming the fields and swamps with his dogs. Often while hunting they would all stop by Mrs. Pinckney's house for a chat and perhaps a bite to eat — even a hungry hound dog was welcome

here. It was on just such an occasion that Billy rode up now and found Mrs. Pinckney trying to collar the horses.

"Hello, Mrs. Pinckney," he said in the very friendliest fashion. "That's hardly work for a woman. Lay off, and let me give you a hand."

"Oh, Billy," she answered. "I must say I am glad to see you. These horses are so spoiled. They're enough to try a body's patience."

Billy jumped down from his own horse and quickly took Daisy and Darling in hand. It wasn't a minute before

22

he had them in the traces and Mrs. Pinckney safely aboard.

"Now you be careful," Billy said, and he gave her a big wink. "Remember the city can be dangerous; it's not like our Coolewahee — and especially, don't take any sass from any of those snooty city ladies."

"Billy, how you do carry on. You'd think I'd never been to town before. I've watched you grow from a pup, and it's me who will decide who needs looking after. I'll be back in a couple of days and tell you all the latest talk."

With that Mrs. Pinckney drove off, and with June the Tiger along, Billy knew she would be safe.

June the Tiger liked a trip almost as much as a bear fight. He would run along beside the buggy and bark, and be barked at, by every dog along the way. Lord knows what June the Tiger was so eternally proud of, but when traveling, his manner was nothing less than pompous. At every dog who challenged the course of the buggy, he would glance down his rather short snoot with a look of utter disdain; then follow with a show of ferocity which a good poker player might call a bluff, but which few dogs were willing to challenge. By and large he kept close by the wagon, but there were always numerous sallies into the woods to chase something or other, which was never caught, and probably never existed in the first place.

Unfortunately for June the Tiger there was one disagreeable aspect of a trip to town. He was looked upon with complete horror by Mrs. Pinckney's friends. They thought his country manners scandalous and his rather wild appearance a disgrace. Indeed, if Tiger was possessed of any virtue, it went entirely unnoticed among these ladies of the city. He was always required to remain on the porch, where he and the house dogs would eye each other through the screen door in a manner which paid no tribute to the friendship of their masters.

Tiger, however, was a master at turning bad fortune into good, and one day while Mrs. Pinckney was having her morning coffee at the home of Mrs. Wilhelmina Cain the opportunity presented itself to make a dash inside. Tiger may have been small, but he didn't carry any small number of fleas, and those he did carry were as rough and tough a bunch as ever cocked a dog's ear. As soon as the fleas got inside the house they all hopped off June the Tiger and fell upon the house dogs. Tiger then scooted out the back door, and quite satisfied with himself, waited for Mrs. Pinckney to finish her visit.

The house dogs, however, lived for a week in an agony of scratching, until finally Mrs. Cain had them taken outside and washed in a tub with hot water and

24

black soap. That bath did those dogs a lot of good too. It not only got rid of the fleas but a lot of uppityness as well.

Chapter Five

Mrs. Pinckney's trip to town was a huge success. At least a ton of tea was poured at dozens of parties given in her honor, and all the old bachelors really outdid themselves in vying for her attention. However, while she was in the city there occurred a storm back at Coolewahee of an intensity rarely seen in those parts. It was one of those strange visitations from the tropics which, though spawned at sea, will often attack the coastal regions with an unnatural vengeance. How long this terrible storm had wandered at sea no one knows, but in this lonely bit of swamp it chose to vent its dying fury.

The sound of such a storm is not of this world, and indeed it has been said that the devil himself walked abroad that night. If the devil did not, Old Scratch certainly did. For as the wind howled, the bear worked himself into a terrible temper, and slowly, but with a determination that exceeded even the wild night, he made his way out of the swamp and up the little road that led to Mrs. Pinckney's house.

The huge bear was black, as black as cave mud, and

now, as he moved silently through the night like some ancient ghost, he inhaled all the fury of the storm. When he reached the edge of the swamp he stopped for a long, long moment.

Often the most violent noise will produce a feeling of intense quiet, and so it was tonight. Through the raging storm there prevailed an eerie stillness, and as Old Scratch rose to his full height against the midnight sky, none could mistake that woeful chant:

> *June, June the Tiger*
> *June, June be wary . . .*

It was a sound that on any other night would have brought June the Tiger a-running, but tonight it could not be, and the bear, turning his ear to the wind but hearing nothing, moved a little closer toward Mrs. Pinckney's house. It was a strange and frightening sight, that huge black mass moving slowly up the road, pausing every few steps, testing the air, then letting forth in ever increasing volume that unearthly song:

> *June, June the Tiger*
> *June, June be wary . . .*

The sound seemed to have a life of its own and as it

swirled through the night it would grow or diminish, and return in a thousand tonal variations. When Old Scratch reached the little gate, whitewashed ever so carefully, he shook it furiously, then once again that demoniacal wail:

June, June the Tiger
June, June be wary . . .

Scratch was mad, mad like you and I don't know about. I mean, he wouldn't have howdyed a preacher on Sunday. Why, he smashed that little gate no different than if he were slapping a mosquito, and plowed across the yard like he was breaking up new ground. In less time than it takes to tell about it, Mrs. Pinckney's garden was nothing but bear tracks and Scratch was through the door and into the house.

When the old bear realized that June the Tiger was definitely not there, he really went to work on that house. I guess he broke up everything in sight and what he didn't break up he ate up. Most any bear is liable to get a bit overanxious in a kitchen with no one around to make him mind his manners, but this bear went plumb crazy.

As you know, Mrs. Pinckney was quite the cook, and her pantry was full of enough food to feed a regiment, and of a quality to tempt the most fastidious bear. But this bear was certainly no gourmet; I daresay he would eat anything from horseflies to cactus spurs and probably didn't know the difference. A taste for ham, though, is not hard to cultivate, and in this Scratch showed a flexibility not unworthy of his appetite.

I suppose there are those among you who won't believe one bear could eat a whole pantry full of hams, sides of bacon, sacks of flour, and jars of preserves; but I'm here to tell you that if he didn't eat it all he ate most of it, and what he didn't eat he scattered over everything

28

including himself. The efforts of his gluttony completely destroyed the tidy kitchen; the terrible bear raked every shelf and cupboard until nothing remained but heaps of broken silver and china.

When at last he had eaten his fill, Scratch began to wander about in search of more mischief. There was no moon, and the house was as black as pitch, but the bear's eyes glowed with a villainous light as he reeled and crashed about. It was a bad piece of luck for Mrs. Pinckney when the bear's heavy body stumbled against the stairway that led to the upstairs bedroom and the wonderful feather bed. Slowly and clumsily Scratch climbed the fragile steps, and when he found the bed it was as if he sensed the great value in which it was held, for he roared horribly and attacked it with all his strength. Ahrrrrrrrrrrrrrrrrr! . . . His great claws ripped and raked until a mass of swirling feathers was all that remained of the handsome heirloom. But the huge beast, his mind dulled from his recent feast, had now created a monster his own equal. The wind blowing through the open doors whipped the feathers into a regular blizzard. Those feathers that didn't stick to his fur went up his nose, and when he began to sneeze he looked and sounded for all the world like some giant rooster. The bear howled in panic as he groped about seeking to avoid the smothering mass. He had had more than enough, and when finally he escaped into the night his sense of relief was second only to the pleasure he felt in his night's work.

The storm was now beginning to subside, and before long first light would touch the eastern sky. Old Scratch stood looking into the night, his swayback and distended paunch adding a grotesque touch to his appearance that nature had not intended. The huge meal had been almost more than his body could stand, and he made only halting progress as he began to wind his way along the road. Forced to walk upright because of the great weight in his stomach, his gait was unsteady, like that of a drunken man, and it was many hours before he fell asleep among the roots of an ancient cypress deep in the heart of the swamp.

Chapter Six

Mrs. Pinckney didn't hurry on her way home. It was a lovely day and the countryside was too beautiful to pass quickly. Daisy and Darling knew the way and at their own pace would just reach Five Mile Creek at lunchtime. Here a rest in the shade awaited them, and Mrs. Pinckney and June the Tiger would have a picnic in the glade.

What a picnic it was. Mrs. Pinckney was quite the one for ceremony — always a white cloth on the ground, knives, forks, plates — no different than if the old General himself were stopping by for dinner. The squirrels thought it a bit strange, but Mrs. Pinckney thought it just fine, and June the Tiger never complained about fried chicken and hoppin' john, no matter how it was served.

There was little about Five Mile Creek to bring it to the attention of the world, but it was there all the same. Sassafras and willow grew along its banks, and there was seldom a time when a cane pole and a can of worms would not fill the frying pan. If one were both quiet and patient it was possible to see turtles sunning on logs along the water's edge — they would plop in at the least disturbance — a great blue heron wading in the shallows, wood ducks nesting in a hollow tree, an otter playing, or a raccoon searching for crayfish and spring lizards. It was also possible to see nothing — only to be seen.

The little glade where Mrs. Pinckney had her lunch always seemed so quiet. Sunlit fields are often busy, but here was only the gentle moss and the delicate scent of bay and jasmine.

It was well into the afternoon before Mrs. Pinckney left the glade, and she had to hurry to be home before dark. The fields were full of black-eyed susans, and a partridge was happily whistling to his mate. There was no way Mrs. Pinckney could have known what had happened to her little house. Even the noisy cries of the crows feasting on the scraps of scattered food did not give her warning. It was a sad moment indeed when she drove up into the yard, only to see that everything she loved had been treated so unkindly. Daisy and Darling came to a halt, and with faltering steps Mrs. Pinckney bravely got out of the buggy. The house had been turned inside out, her pantry was empty, and the precious little things she had treasured for so many years were all broken and thrown about.

Mrs. Pinckney was at first horrified, then as she saw the extent of the damage, horror turned to anger, but in the end both of these feelings gave way to a desperate helplessness which she had never before experienced. She

had a brave heart, and although trouble usually passed her by, she could look it straight in the eye if the need arose. But when she saw those feathers, and knew that the wonderful old bed was ruined, it was simply too much for one so unaccustomed to mistreatment. Not knowing what to do, and with a broken heart as well, she just sat down on the front steps and began to cry. "Boo-hooh, boo-hooh-hooh, oh, boo-hooh." Nothing could stop Mrs. Pinckney's sobs, and as night began to fall, she just sat and cried, and cried, and cried.

Chapter Seven

Well, Mrs. Pinckney continued to cry, and June the Tiger was quite beside himself. I don't mind telling you that the situation did not look good. Things might have gone badly indeed if Billy the Bull had not come riding up just then. And a proud sight he was, too; straight and tall in the saddle like the gentleman he was.

As soon as the storm was over Billy had decided to ride by Mrs. Pinckney's house to see if there had been any damage. The road was in bad shape and he was forced to clear fallen trees along the way. The cottage had been through hurricanes before, but he was sure the livestock would need attention. He did not expect Mrs. Pinckney to have returned, so his surprise was doubly great when he found her sitting on the front steps crying, and the house and yard a wreck.

"Oh, Billy," Mrs. Pinckney sobbed, "just look what some awful man has done to my house. Everything is all broken up and my feather bed is ruined. I can't imagine why anyone would do such a frightful thing. Oh, boo-hooh-hooh."

Well sir, Billy the Bull was not the one for long speeches, and he didn't make one now, but he did give Mrs. Pinckney a big hug and a kiss for to dry the tears away. Billy could look as proud as a hawk, and he had a temper to match. He was in a rage when he walked into

the cottage. It didn't take him long to size up exactly what had happened during the night. If Scratch had been handy I think Billy would have lit into him barefisted. Billy was mad all right, but he was one for a tight spot and he knew all there was to know about bears, and he decided to fix Old Scratch's hide once and for all.

"Now Mrs. Pinckney," said Billy, "you just leave off that boo-hoohing right now. I'll not be having that. What's done is done, and I never saw a piece of good come from crying. What's more, I know a deal more about bears than I do about men, and this was surely a bear, and a big one, too, that was here last night. From the looks of that house I would say it was Old Scratch that did the dirty work. He's the most dangerous bear in these parts, and it's probably a lucky thing you weren't at home when he decided to come calling."

Billy did know about bears, and he had no intention of letting this one get a head start on him, but first he had to look after Mrs. Pinckney. She could not stay in the little house until things were straightened out a bit, and as night was coming on, there was no time for that now.

It was early evening by the time Billy got Mrs. Pinckney packed into the buggy and off on the short trip to his mother's house. Mrs. Pinckney felt much better, now that Billy was with her. She and Billy's mother were old friends, and she knew she would be welcome there for as long as she wished to stay. The trip was not a long one, and it was a lovely summer evening. The moonflowers were beginning to stir, and the bats and nighthawks were busy vying for the night's mosquito crop. Billy was in a high pitch of excitement, and as he drove the team, even Daisy and Darling seemed to catch the spirit of the night and hurried along faster than usual. All the dogs and Billy's horse followed along behind, and it was a noisy party indeed that drove up into the yard of the old plantation home. Here Mrs. Pinckney would be safe, and Billy could make final preparations for the night's hunt.

Chapter Eight

A bear hunt anytime is nothing to yawn about, but in the middle of the night with only the moon and a pine torch to light the way, the combination of an angry bear and a dark swamp is enough to make anyone's heart beat a little faster than usual. Yes, there was plenty of excitement all right, and you may lay to it that the dogs were right in the thick of things. When June the Tiger realized they were going after the bear that night he went into a state of uncontrolled glee. I'm sure no sane dog ever acted that way before. A bucketful of steaks would not have kept him still. He growled and yipped, and lay on his back and kicked his legs in the air. He carried on so during the trip to Billy's mother's house that by the time they were halfway there he was so coated with black mud and cockleburs that he looked like a moving briar patch. He

attacked one mud puddle with such ferocity that a fat frog swallowed his tongue in his hurry to avoid the raging dog, and a little farther down the road he bit a log so hard that his teeth got stuck, and Billy had to stop and pry him loose.

There's no disputing that June the Tiger was ready to go, but he wasn't the only dog going hunting that night, and most folks, not knowing what you and I know, would have said that compared to Billy's dogs, June the Tiger was not much.

Billy had a couple of beauts all right. I reckon they could smell down, run down, and chase up a tree most any critter in Coolewahee Swamp. The strike dog's name was Clippity-Clang. He was all nose, ears and feet, but he got more use out of those parts than seemed natural even to a hound dog. Clippity-Clang was mostly black and tan, or tan and black, depending on which way you looked at it, and he had but two pleasures in life — hunting and sleeping. When he wasn't doing one, he was surely at the other, and it's hard to say at which of these noble pursuits he excelled the most. When Clippity-Clang was sleeping, nothing, I mean nobody or no amount of commotion, could disturb him. He could flop down in a shady spot with the flies buzzin' around, and look dead as any possum. He might get up once in a while to lap at the water pail, or at suppertime to wolf down a few hunks of cornbread soaked in bacon grease, but for the most part he didn't move and to all appearances couldn't have if he wanted to.

But show the glint of a rifle barrel or blow a hunting horn, and that dog would come alive like he was high on moonshine. He was lop-eared and knock-kneed but once he was moving, Clippity-Clang could outrun and outsmell any dog in the district. He was surely a phenomenon. The country people said that when Billy was hunting, Clippity-Clang would run plumb up in the next county and chase all the varmints down to him. That dog could smell where a bear had been last week and could speak in tongues when he was on a fresh track. He would start with a series of yelps and end in a howl that would frighten the devil. Yes-sir-ree-bob, he was something else, and Billy loved him like a child!

Then there was Bullwah. He wasn't a hound — more bulldog than anything else, I guess; but what he lacked in speed and nose he made up for with pugnacious determination. He would follow along after Clippity-Clang as best he could, panting like an old locomotive and trying hard to keep from falling in a gator hole. He would bark whenever he could, but it was a disappointing effort and did not do his bravery justice. Only when whatever it was they were chasing was caught up with did Bullwah show his true worth. He could shake the eyes out of most any varmint and hang on to a bear till it hollered for help. Bullwah had more courage than sense, but all in all he and Clippity-Clang made a fine pair of dogs. June the Tiger was traveling in good company that night.

Chapter Nine

Billy wasn't long in getting ready. Rifle, powder, shot, his hunting knife, and a couple of pine knots to use for torches were all he needed. He had left his horse saddled, since

42

he intended to ride back to Mrs. Pinckney's and go on foot from there. The dogs were near fit to be tied in their excitement, and as Billy mounted and turned in the saddle for a final farewell to his mother and Mrs. Pinckney, the noise of their barking all but drowned out the ladies' cries to please be careful.

Billy placed his long curved hunting horn to his lips and its hoarse cry announced to all that the hunt had begun. The night air had helped to clear his head of the anger he'd experienced earlier and now, as he posted along the sandy road, he calmly planned the night's adventure. It was a big swamp, and the hunt was likely to last all night, and even into the next day. Once the dogs picked up the scent of the bear, they would run on ahead, and it would be up to Billy to follow along as best he could. Scratch knew Coolewahee like the back of his paw and would give them all the slip if ever he decided to run for it. It would be up to the dogs to jump him, then hold him at bay long enough, without getting themselves killed, for Billy to catch up and take a shot.

It was only a short ride back to the cottage, and when Billy got there he stabled his horse and lit one of the pine torches. Around the house, where the ground was most exposed, the rain had washed out most of the tracks, and all the scent. Billy quickly saw that if he were to pick up the trail at all, it would have to be at the edge of the swamp, where the dense foliage had dissipated some of the force of the rain. He started down the road with his gun slung on his back, the torch held above his head, his eyes on the ground in front of him, and the dogs whimpering and searching frantically for some trace of the scent.

Where the road reached the swamp it narrowed and became nothing more than a foot trail. Here, sure enough, Billy found the tracks of the great bear. They were huge, bigger than any Billy had ever seen before. Some of the tracks were so deep that the shadows cast by the torch made them look like black holes in the surface of the road. Others had filled with water, and a grown man could fully have placed both his boots in some of the resulting puddles. It was enough to make a brave man go back — but Billy pushed on.

Soon after entering the swamp, they came to places where the bear had brushed up against trees and bushes, and here the keen nose of Clippity-Clang picked up the scent. As soon as Clippity-Clang smelled the bear, he let out a howl that was pure hound dog and all business. He pointed his nose toward the sky, gave a couple of short yelps, and ended with a series of howls that were music to Billy's ears . . . Roof-roof-ahoooooooh! Roof-a-hoooooooh! Ahoooooooh! Ahoooooooh! . . . Clippity-

Clang took off at a full run with Bullwah, June the Tiger, and Billy following along as best they could.

When Scratch left Mrs. Pinckney's he had headed straight for his favorite lair in the area of the swamp known as Sawbuck Island. It was only at unusually high water that the Sawbuck was actually an island, but at all times it was a difficult place to reach. The island was surrounded on three sides by boggy savannahs and on the fourth by Whooping Crane Pond. Anyone approaching Sawbuck Island had either to come by boat or to cross several hundred yards of savannah, which abounded with knife-sharp saw grass.

Scratch lay sprawled in a deep sleep among the roots of an old cypress. His breathing was heavy, and he snorted and snored from the burden of his recent feast. When Clippity-Clang howled he woke up. The bear's head was groggy, but he recognized the sound of dog and listened more closely to be sure it was not June the Tiger.

Clippity-Clang howled again . . . Ahoooooooh! . . . . . . Ahoooooooh! . . . This time Scratch heard it clearly. It was not June the Tiger. The old bear wasn't scared of any hound, that's for sure. He'd fought with plenty of them, and most were now gone to wherever the good Lord looks after poor dead dogs. Clippity-Clang wasn't likely to be any different, so with a satisfied grunt, and a great heave of his huge body, Old Scratch went on back to sleep.

Chapter Ten

Ahooooooooh! Ahooooooooh! Ahooooooooh! Ahooooooooh! Clippity-Clang was still at it, and even though the scent was now a day old he hadn't lost the trail more'n a couple of times — once where the bear had swum a creek and again at Dinner Pond Lake. Billy was worried, though.

They still hadn't caught up to the bear, and come daylight that critter just might get a notion to do some travelin'. Where to? Only Scratch would know that, I guess, but if it did happen it would more than likely mean the end of the hunt.

The trail now led down toward the old Indian burying ground. It was right at the great shell ring that Bullwah started acting strange. The seashells had been placed in a perfect circle on the graves thousands of years ago by Indian holy men. It was believed the bones of the dead chiefs could still work magic, and folks hunted them to cure both swamp fever and the yellowjack. It was here that Bullwah stopped, put his nose to the ground, turned around a couple of times, then his hair stood up and his whole body began to twitch like he'd been bit by a moccasin. All of a sudden he threw his head back and began to holler. It sounded like the voodoo curse all right, but it wasn't. Bullwah had picked up the scent.

Ahrooof! Ahrooof! Ahrooof! Ahroof! . . . The bark was a low sound that came from deep within his chest. When Billy heard it he knew the dogs were getting close. Old Scratch heard it, too, but paid no attention. It would take more than a voodoo curse from a bulldog to budge him.

Clippity-Clang kept howling. Ahoooooooh! A-hooooooooh! Ahoooooooh! . . . Now Bullwah: Ahrooof! Ahrooof! . . . and all the time June the Tiger was like to have a fit. He knew that bear was there somewhere but he couldn't smell him yet. Just give him a chance and he'd have Old Scratch's head where his feet ought to be and

the hair flying off him like rain from a shook branch. In the meantime he'd run into a good half the trees in the swamp, swum seventeen dozen creeks, and been snapped at by at least two hundred alligators. Was it worth it? Listen! I'm here to tell you that to June the Tiger it was like Christmas, Thanksgiving, and his birthday all rolled into one.

It was just breaking dawn when the dogs finally reached the savannah surrounding Sawbuck Island. The moss hung dripping with early dew, and even the most brilliant colors could only be seen as varying shades of gray. Clippity-Clang got there first, and he stopped to wait for the other dogs to catch up. It was here, practically in Scratch's backyard, that June the Tiger finally picked up the scent, and when he did, all three dogs took off across the savannah together with Clippity-Clang in the lead going Ahooooooooh! Ahooooooooh! . . . followed by Bullwah . . . Ahrooof! Ahrooof! . . . and on top of all that, June the Tiger. There is no way any description could do justice to the sounds *that* dog was making, but at the very least it sounded like a whole yard full of dogs, each with his tail being stepped on: Arururururururururu! Arururururururururu! Arururururururururu! . . . It was a combination of snarls, yips, and howls that didn't sound much like a dog, or anything else for that matter. "Original." That's what Sammy Bailey used to call that bark. "Original."

Scratch hadn't paid much attention to the other dogs but when he heard June the Tiger he started up in a hurry. The old bear knew he was in for a fight he hadn't counted on, and he roared a great horrible roar: Ahrrrrrrrrrrrr!

The dogs were already on the island, and at that very moment Clippity-Clang broke through the underbrush into the clearing in which the bear now stood, reared his full height in the morning mist. Clippity-Clang was running so fast that he hadn't seen the bear until it was too late, and now he skidded to a halt not a foot in front of him. Scratch roared again: Ahrrrrrrrrrrrr! . . . Life and death hung in the balance. In another instant the bear would have crushed Clippity-Clang with one swipe of a huge paw had it not been that, as if from nowhere, there shot through the air a ball of fur and yelps that hit the bear full flush in the chest and knocked him backwards to the ground.

Need I say that that ball of yelping fur was none other than June the Tiger? His short legs couldn't make it through the saw grass quite as quick as Clippity-Clang's, but I reckon he got there soon enough, and when he saw

Clippity-Clang lying on the ground with Scratch reared over him, he covered the last twenty yards in one leap.

No sooner was Scratch down than June the Tiger was on top of him. He lit into that bear's stomach like a swarm of July mosquitos. However, a bear's stomach is not the safest of places, and with another horrible roar Scratch caught Tiger a kick that sent him soaring skyward with a force sure to clear the treetops. With June the Tiger out of the way Scratch quickly regained his feet and turned all his attention to the other dogs.

Bullwah had been belly-high in mud all the way across the savannah. He looked so much like part of the swamp that Scratch hadn't even seen him. But Bullwah was only waiting for a good chance, and when he got it he leaped in and took a hold of the bear's neck. It was a good hold and the old bear roared horribly and tried to shake him loose . . . Ahrrrrrrrrrrrr! . . . Clippity-Clang kept howling Ahoooooooh! Ahoooooooh! Ahoooooooh! . . . Still far away in the swamp Billy could hear the fight. He was running for all he was worth and only hoped the dogs could hold on till he got there.

Whether June the Tiger was simply dazed by his fall, or whether it just took him a while to land I don't know, but in either case he was gone for quite a spell, and by the time he got back to the fight poor Clippity-Clang had been knocked senseless, and Scratch had Bullwah in a squeeze that would soon have meant the end of him. They were two good dogs, but Old Scratch was part monster and part devil, and it hadn't taken him long to get the upper hand. But Tiger's courage was still undaunted, and he flew at the bear again with all his might; Ahrrrrrrrrrrrr! . . . Scratch roared. Arurururururururu! Arurururururururu! June the Tiger was still barking.

Scratch knew that to deal with June the Tiger he

would have to let loose of Bullwah. This he did, and the half-crushed bulldog dropped gasping to the ground like so much grits in a sack. Scratch then came down on all fours to meet June the Tiger's charge. He slapped wildly with his huge paws in an attempt to catch the speedy dog, but June the Tiger was both everywhere and nowhere. He swarmed over Scratch like ants after a grasshopper, and though he could do little real damage, his bites were both painful and frustrating to the bear. Scratch roared more terribly than ever . . . Ahrrrrrrrrrrrr! Ahrrrrrrrrrrrr!

June the Tiger had the bear turning in circles all right, but even at that, I'm not sure how long he could have kept it up. Old Scratch had his back to the wall, and here in the swamp he fought with greater confidence. There is a limit beyond which courage alone is no longer enough, and I fear that June the Tiger would shortly have been done for had not Billy the Bull arrived when he did.

Billy had had a tough time of it. His clothes were in shreds, and he was so scratched and cut about the face and hands as to have lost considerable blood. He'd been forced to run most of the night in his efforts to keep up with the dogs, and when he arrived at the clearing he was weak and exhausted.

Neither the bear nor June the Tiger saw Billy as he knelt beside the clearing loading his gun. Billy had done his best to keep his powder dry, but he wasn't sure he'd been successful. He'd swum or waded many a creek that night, and it took only a few drops of water to render both the powder and the gun useless. As he rammed the ball home he could see that June the Tiger was tiring in his efforts to avoid the bear.

It was difficult to draw a bead on Old Scratch as he whirled and turned in his fight with June the Tiger. Billy kept coming in closer until he was within a few yards. He

would only have one shot before the bear saw him and charged, but when he squeezed the trigger and heard the gun go off, he knew the shot had found its mark. Old Scratch never heard the crack of the rifle nor felt the sting of the ball. The bullet had penetrated his heart, and he sank instantly to the ground, stone dead.

Chapter Eleven

June the Tiger was sure he'd killed the bear, and some of the Coolewahee people still say it is so. If he didn't kill him, he carried on no different than if he had, and I'm not sure it makes much difference anyway.

Although hurt too badly to walk, Clippity-Clang and Bullwah were soon revived. On the long trip out of the swamp, Billy carried one dog under each arm. With the great bearskin slung over his shoulders, and with June the Tiger leading the way, they made a strange-looking procession. A hero's welcome awaited them, and as the country people looked on in amazement, Billy blew his horn while June the Tiger danced a jig.

Mrs. Pinckney was quite unflappable; and it was only a short time before she had as good as forgotten all about the bear. Many of her neighbors and friends chipped in and helped repair her house. It didn't look quite the same with a fresh coat of paint, but time soon took care of that. They even got together all the soft feathers they had been saving and made her a new feather bed.

Billy the Bull made a beautiful rug out of the bearskin and gave it to Mrs. Pinckney. She put it in front of the fireplace in the parlor, and for many years afterwards when the nights were wet and stormy, June the Tiger would sleep on that great bearskin rug. It was always a fitful sleep, though, for every so often his whole body would shake and jerk about. Mrs. Pinckney would think he was just chasing rabbits, as the saying goes, but I think *we* know what June the Tiger was dreaming about.